2019   19

To Lily Hudson ~TM

For Migs and Meddy ~ AB

Bloomsbury Publishing, London, New Delhi, New York and Sydney

First published in Great Britain in 2015 by Bloomsbury Publishing Plc
50 Bedford Square, London, WC1B 3DP

Text copyright © Tony Mitton 2015
Illustration copyright © Alison Brown 2015
The moral rights of the author and illustrator have been asserted

A CIP catalogue record for this book is available from the British Library

ISBN 978 1 4088 5333 7 (HB)
ISBN 978 1 4088 5334 4 (PB)

Printed in China by Leo Paper Products, Heshan, Guangdong

1 3 5 7 9 10 8 6 4 2

www.bloomsbury.com

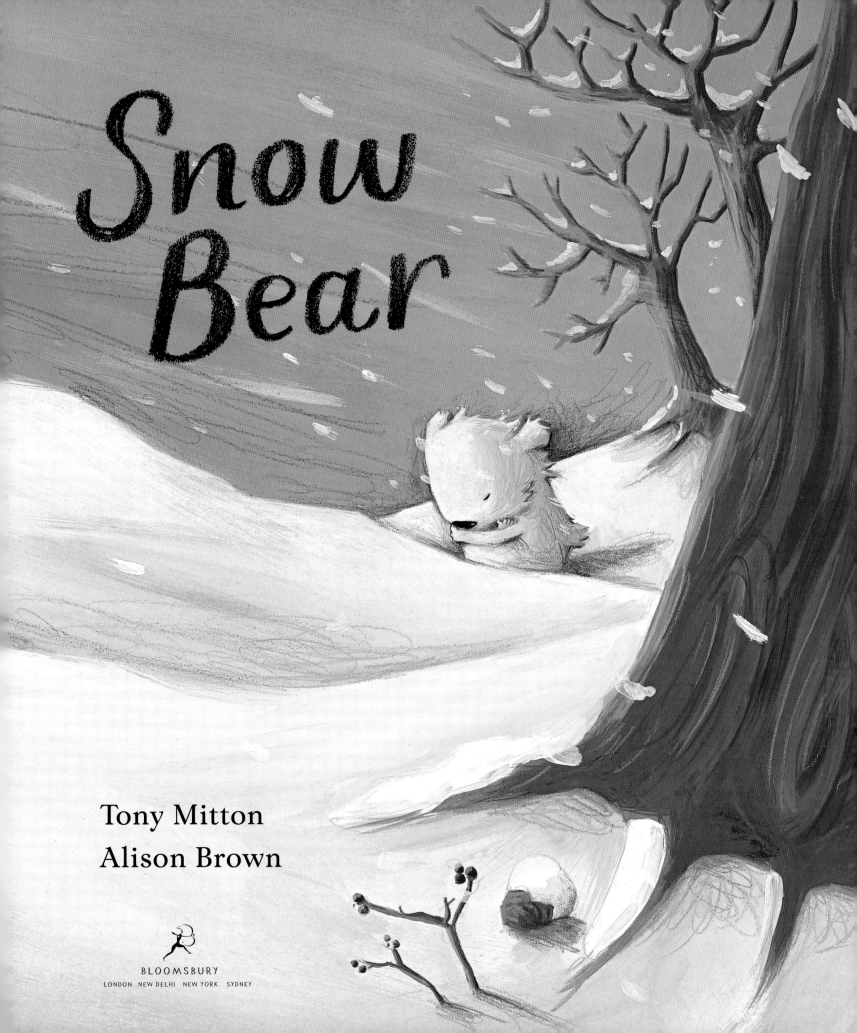

Snow Bear

Tony Mitton

Alison Brown

BLOOMSBURY

LONDON NEW DELHI NEW YORK SYDNEY

Here is a bear who has nowhere to go,
so he's plodding along through the cold winter snow.
Behind him his prints trace a long, weary line,
but ahead the snow's waiting, unbroken and fine.

If you were that poor little shivery bear
you'd want to find comfort and warmth. Yes, but where?

He's spotted a hole, and it's dark, dry and deep.
Perhaps it's a place where a cold bear could sleep?

"Oh, I'm sorry," growls Fox, "but there's no room to spare.
It's my den, and my litter of cubs are down there."

Snow Bear plods on
to a crooked old tree.
There's a warm, cosy hole in it –
could it be free?

But tufty gruff Owl hoots,
"Tu-whit!" and "Tu-whoo!
My chicks are in there
so there's no room for you."

Snow Bear just sighs. Then he trudges along.
"Oh, for a home!" is his sad little song.

But look! A small farmhouse
has come into sight,
a place that looks warm
in this cold world of white.

Perhaps there's a fire,
all glowing and gold,
to cheer a bear up
from the wintery cold.

A chilly breeze ruffles the fur on his cheek,
so Bear tiptoes in as the door gives a creak.

Inside it is warm, for the fire burns bright,
and Snow Bear can see by its flickering light.

There by the window a child stands alone.
No one is with her. She's all on her own.
She looks through the window and out at the snow.
She's a little bit lonely, Bear seems to know.

She turns, for she senses him looking at her.
And there Snow Bear stands with his fluffy white fur.

She gathers him up and she cuddles him tight.
And suddenly Snow Bear feels happy and right.

The little girl teaches him lots of new games.
Then they sit by the fire, gazing into the flames.
The girl gets a book and she reads him a story,
till both of them start feeling sleepy and snorey.

The day's nearly over for girl and for Bear,
so they climb up the rickety, creaky old stair.

The girl takes the bear in her cuddly lap
and they both snuggle down for a midwinter nap.

And that's where we'll leave them, both happily there –
a tired little girl and a weary Snow Bear.
A cold winter day has now come to an end
and a girl and a Snow Bear have both found a friend.